The

PIGEON

TRANSLATED FROM THE GERMAN

BY JOHN E. WOODS

ALFRED A. KNOPF NEW YORK 1988

PATRICK SÜSKIND

The
PIGEON

Library of Congress Cataloging-in-Publication Data

Süskind, Patrick.
The pigeon.

Translation of: Die Taube.
I. Title.
PT2681.U74T3813   1988   833′.914   87-46106
ISBN 0-394-56315-8

The

PIGEON

$\sim$$A$t the time the pigeon affair overtook him, unhinging his life from one day to the next, Jonathan Noel, already past fifty, could look back over a good twenty-year period of total uneventfulness and would never have expected anything of importance could ever overtake him again—other than death someday. And that was perfectly all right with him. For he was not fond of events, and hated outright those that rattled his inner equilibrium and made a muddle of the external arrangements of life.

The majority of such events lay, thank God, far back in the dim, remote years of his childhood and youth, which he no longer had any desire whatever to recall, and when he did, then only with the greatest aversion: On a summer afternoon, in July of 1942, in or near Charenton, as he was returning home from fishing—there had been a thunderstorm that

day with heavy rain, after a long heat wave—
on the way home he had taken off his shoes,
had walked along the warm, wet asphalt with
bare feet and splashed through the puddles, an
indescribable delight . . . he had come home
from fishing, then, and had run into the
kitchen, expecting to find his mother there
cooking, and his mother was nowhere to be
seen, all that was to be seen was her apron,
hanging over the back of the chair. His mother
was gone, his father said, she had had to go
away for a long time on a trip. They had
taken her away, said the neighbors, they had
taken her first to the Vélodrome d'Hiver and
then out to the camp at Drancy, from there it
was off to the east, and no one ever came back
from there. And Jonathan comprehended
nothing of this event, it had totally confused
him, and then a few days later his father had
vanished as well, and Jonathan and his
younger sister suddenly found themselves in
a train heading south, and the next thing were
being led across a meadow by total strangers
and then tugged through a stretch of woods

4

and once more put on a train heading to the south, far away, farther than they could ever comprehend, and an uncle, whom they had never seen before, picked them up in Cavaillon and brought them to his farm near the village of Puget in the valley of the Durance and kept them hidden there until the end of the war. Then he put them to work in his vegetable fields.

In the early fifties—Jonathan was beginning to take to the farm worker's life—the uncle had demanded that he report for military duty, and Jonathan obediently signed up for three years. The first year, he had been occupied solely with getting used to the nuisances of life in a horde, in a barracks. The second year, he was shipped off to Indochina. The greatest part of the third year he spent in the hospital, recovering from a shot in the foot and one in the leg and from amoebic dysentery. When he returned to Puget in the spring of 1954, his sister had vanished, had emigrated to Canada, people said. The uncle now demanded that Jonathan wed posthaste,

and that it be to a girl named Marie Bac-
couche from the neighboring village of Lauris;
and Jonathan, who had never seen the girl before, stoutly did as he was told, indeed did it
gladly, for although he had only an imperfect
notion of married life, he nevertheless hoped
that he would finally find himself in a state
of monotone serenity and uneventfulness, the
only state, in fact, for which he longed. But
within a mere four months, Marie gave birth
to a boy and that same autumn bolted with
a Tunisian fruit merchant from Marseille.

Drawing on all these episodes, Jonathan
Noel came to the conclusion that you cannot
depend on people, and that you can live in
peace only if you keep them at arm's length.
And because he had now also become the
laughingstock of the village—which disturbed
him not because of the laughter, but because
of the public attention he was attracting—for
the first time in his life he made a decision on
his own: He went to the Crédit Agricole, with-
drew his savings, packed his bag, and headed
for Paris.

Then he had a double stroke of luck. He found work as a guard at a bank in the rue de Sèvres, and he found lodgings, a so-called *chambre de bonne* on the seventh floor of a building in the rue de la Planche. You got to the room by way of a back courtyard, the narrow service stairway, and a cramped hallway sparely lit by one window. Two dozen small rooms, each numbered in gray paint, lay along this hallway, and at the far end was number 24, Jonathan's room. It measured eleven feet two inches in length by seven feet three inches in width and was eight feet two inches high, and its sole conveniences were a bed, a table, a chair, a light bulb, and a clothes hook, nothing more. Not until the sixties did rewiring make it possible to plug in a hot plate and a space heater, and the plumbing was also redone to provide the room with its own basin and hot-water heater. Until then, all the residents of the garret had eaten their meals cold—that is, if they didn't use an outlawed alcohol burner—slept in cold rooms, and washed their socks, their few dishes, and themselves with cold water in a single basin out in the hall, right next to the door of the shared toilet. All of which did not bother Jonathan. He was not looking for comfort, but for secure lodgings that belonged to him and him alone, that protected him against life's unpleasant surprises and from which no one could ever drive him away again. And upon entering room number 24 for the first time, he had known at once: This is it, this is what you've really always wanted, this is where you'll stay. (Just the way it happens to other people, or so they say, with so-called love at first sight, when in a flash someone realizes that some woman he has never seen before is the woman of his life, that he will possess her and remain with her until the end of his days.)

Jonathan Noel rented this room for five thousand old francs a month, left it every morning to go to work in the nearby rue de Sèvres, returned in the evening with bread, charcuterie, apples, and cheese, ate, slept, and was happy. On Sunday he did not leave the room at all, but cleaned it instead and fitted his bed with fresh sheets. And so he lived, in peace and contentment, year in, year out, decade after decade.

Certain extraneous matters changed during this time—the amount of rent, for instance, the kinds of tenants. In the fifties, a good many servant girls had lived in the other rooms and young married couples and a few pensioners. Later on, you often saw Spaniards, Portuguese, North Africans moving in and out. From the end of the sixties on, students predominated. Finally, not all twenty-four rooms were rented anymore. Many stood empty or were used for storage or occasionally for guests of residents who lived in the elegant apartments below. Over the years, Jonathan's number 24 had become a comfortable dwelling, comparatively speaking. He had bought himself a new bed, fashioned a built-in cupboard, laid a gray carpet over its eighty-one square feet, done the niche for cooking and washing in beautiful red oilskin wallpaper. He owned a radio, a television set, and an iron. He no longer hung his provisions out the window in sacks as before, but instead kept them in a tiny refrigerator under the washbasin, so that now his butter did not melt nor his ham dry out, even during the hottest summer. At the head of his bed he had erected a bookcase, in which stood no fewer than seventeen books, viz. a medical pocket dictionary in three volumes, several lovely illustrated books on Cro-Magnon man, the art of Bronze Age casting, the ancient Egyptians, the Etruscans, and the French Revolution, a book on sailing ships, one on flags, one on the fauna of the tropics, two novels by Alexandre Dumas *père*, the memoirs of Saint-Simon, a casserole cookbook, the *Petit Larousse*, and the *Handbook of Security and Guard Personnel with Special Reference to Regulations concerning the Use of the Service Pistol*. Under his bed were stored a dozen bottles of red wine, among them a bottle of Château Cheval-Blanc *grand cru classé*, which he was saving for retirement day in 1998. An ingenious system of lighting allowed Jonathan to sit and read his newspaper in three different places in the room—that is, at the foot and head of his bed as well as at the table—without ever being blinded and with never a shadow falling on the paper.

As a result of all these many acquisitions, the room had of course become smaller still, growing inwardly, as it were, like an oyster encrusted with mother-of-pearl, and in its diverse sophisticated installations resembled more a ship's cabin or a luxurious Pullman compartment than a simple *chambre de bonne*. But its essential character had been maintained down through those thirty years: It was and would remain Jonathan's island of security in a world of insecurity, his refuge, his beloved—yes, for she received him with a tender embrace each evening when he returned home, she offered warmth and protection, she nourished both body and soul, was always there when he needed her and did not desert him. She was in point of fact the only thing that had proved dependable in his life. And therefore he had never for a moment thought of leaving her, not even now, though he was al-

11

ready over fifty and occasionally found it an effort to climb so many stairs, and though his salary would have allowed him to rent a regular apartment with its own kitchen, its own toilet and bath. He remained true to his beloved, was even in the process of strengthening his bonds to her, and hers to him. He wanted to make their relationship inviolable for all time by buying her. He had already signed a contract with Madame Lassalle, the owner. It was to cost him fifty-five thousand new francs. He had already paid forty-seven thousand. The remaining eight thousand were due at the end of the year. And then she would finally be his and nothing in the world would ever be able to separate them—him, Jonathan, and his beloved room—one from the other, until death did them part.

That was the state of things when, in August 1984, on a Friday morning, the affair with the pigeon occurred.

Jonathan had just got up. As he did every morning, he had put on his slippers and bathrobe so that he could visit the shared toilet before shaving. Prior to opening the door, he laid an ear to its panel and listened to hear if anyone was in the hall. He did not relish meeting his fellow tenants, particularly not in the morning in pajamas and bathrobe, and least of all on the way to the toilet. Finding the toilet occupied would have been unpleasant enough; but the idea of meeting another tenant *at the door* of the toilet was nothing short of a nightmare of embarrassment. It had happened to him just one single time, in the summer of 1959, twenty-five years before, and he shuddered to think back on it: the simultaneous shock of each at the sight of the other, the simultaneous loss of anonymity while on a mission demanding absolute ano-nymity, the simultaneous shrinking back and readvancing, the simultaneous reeling off of courtesies: please, after you, oh no, after you, monsieur, I'm in no hurry at all, no, you first, I insist—and all of it in pajamas! No, he never wanted to experience it again, nor had he experienced it again, thanks to his

13

prophylactic ear-to-the-door. By listening, he could see through the door out into the hallway. He knew every noise on the floor. He could interpret every crack, every click, every soft ripple or rustle, the very silence itself. And he knew—now, with his ear to the door for only a couple of seconds—he was quite sure that no one was in the hall, that the toilet was unoccupied, that everyone was still asleep. With his left hand he turned the knob of the security lock, with his right the knop of the spring lock, the bolt slipped back, he pulled with a soft jerk, and the door swung open.

He had almost set his foot across the threshold, had already raised the foot, his left, his leg was in the act of stepping—when he saw it. It was sitting before his door, not eight inches from the threshold, in the pale reflection of dawn that came through the window. It was crouched there, with red, taloned feet on the oxblood tiles of the hall and in sleek, blue-gray plumage: the pigeon.

It had laid its head to one side and was glaring at Jonathan with its left eye. This eye, a small, circular disc, brown with a black center, was dreadful to behold. It was like a button sewn onto the feathers of the head, lashless, browless, quite naked, turned quite shamelessly to the world and monstrously open; at the same time, however, there was something guarded and devious in that eye; and yet likewise it seemed to be neither open nor guarded, but rather quite simply lifeless, like the lens of a camera that swallows all external light and allows nothing to shine back out of its interior. No luster, no shimmer lay in that eye, not a spark of anything alive. It was an eye without sight. And it glared at Jonathan.

He was frightened to death—that was probably how he would have described the moment later on, but that would not have been correct, because the fear came only later. He was, rather, amazed to death.

Perhaps for five, perhaps for ten seconds— to him it seemed like forever—he stood there at the threshold of his door as if frozen, hand on the knob, foot lifted for stepping out,

15

and could move neither forward nor backward. Then some small movement occurred. It might have been that the pigeon shifted its weight from one foot to the other, that it just ruffled itself a little—at any rate, a brief jolt went through its body, and at the same time the two lids snapped together over its eye, one from below, one from above, not real lids either, more like some kind of rubbery flaps that swallowed up the eye like two lips emerging from nowhere. For a moment it vanished. And only now did fear jerk its way through Jonathan, his hair standing on end from pure terror. With a single bound he leaped back into his room and slammed the door, before the pigeon's eye had reopened. He turned the security lock, staggered the three steps to the bed, sat down trembling, his heart pounding wildly. His brow was ice cold, and from his nape all the way down his spine he could feel sweat breaking out.

His first thought was that he would suffer a heart attack or a stroke or at least black out;

he was at the right age for all that, he thought, from fifty on it takes only the least little thing to cause such a mishap. And he let himself fall to one side on the bed and pulled the blanket up over his chilled shoulders and waited for the spasms of pain, for the stab in the area of breast and shoulders (he had once read in his medical pocket dictionary that these were the infallible symptoms of a heart attack) or for the slow waning of consciousness. But nothing of the sort happened. The beat of his heart quieted, his blood flowed again regularly through head and limbs, and signs of paralysis, so typical of a stroke, did not appear. Jonathan could move toes and fingers and distort his face with grimaces, a sign that everything was more or less in order, organically, and neurologically speaking.

Instead, a riotous mass of the most random terrors whirled about in his brain like a swarm of black ravens, and in his head was a screaming and a fluttering, and it croaked, "You've had it! You're too old and you've had it, letting yourself be frightened to death by a

17

pigeon, letting a pigeon drive you back into your room, knock you down, hold you prisoner. You will die, Jonathan, you'll die, if not right away, then soon, and your whole life has been a lie, you've made a mess of it, because it's been upended by a pigeon, you must kill it, but you can't kill it, you can't kill a fly, or wait, a fly yes, a fly you can manage or a mosquito or a little bug, but never something warm-blooded, some warm-blooded creature like a pigeon that weighs a pound, you'd gun down a human being first, bang bang, that's fast, just makes a little hole, a quarter-inch thick, that's clean and it's permissible, in self-defense it's permissible, article one in the regulations for armed security personnel, it's required, in fact, not a soul blames you if you shoot down a person, just the opposite, but a pigeon?, how do you shoot down a pigeon?, it flutters around, a pigeon does, so that you can easily miss, it's a gross misdemeanor to shoot at a pigeon, it's forbidden, that leads to confiscation of your service weapon, to loss of your job, you end up in prison if you shoot at a pigeon, no, you can't kill it, but you can't live, live with it either, never, no human being can go on living in the same house with a pigeon, a pigeon is the epitome of chaos and anarchy, a pigeon that whizzes around unpredictably, that sets its claws in you, picks at your eyes, a pigeon that never stops soiling and spreading the filth and havoc of bacteria and meningitis virus, that doesn't just stay alone, one pigeon lures other pigeons, that leads to sexual intercourse and they breed at a frantic pace, a host of pigeons will lay siege, you won't be able to leave your room ever again, will have to starve, will suffocate in your excrement, will have to throw yourself out the window and lie there smashed on the sidewalk, no, you're too much a coward, you'll stay locked up in your room and scream for help, you'll scream for the fire department, for them to come with ladders and rescue you from a pigeon, from a pigeon!, you'll be the laughingstock of the building, the laughingstock of the whole neighborhood, 'look, Monsieur Noel!' they'll shout, and point their fingers at you,

19

'look, Monsieur Noel has to be rescued from a pigeon!' and they'll admit you to a psychiatric clinic: oh Jonathan, Jonathan, your situation is hopeless, you're a lost man, Jonathan!"

Such were the screamings and croakings in his head, and Jonathan was so bewildered and desperate that he did something that he had not done since childhood days—that is, in his agony he folded his hands to pray, and he prayed, "My God, my God, why hast thou forsaken me? Why dost thou punish me so? Our Father, who art in heaven, save me from this pigeon, amen!" This was, as we can see, no orderly prayer; what he offered up was more like the stammered, patchwork fragments of something recalled from a rudimentary religious education. But it helped nevertheless, for it demanded a certain measure of concentration of the mind and so banished the tangle of his thoughts. Something else helped him still more. He had hardly spoken his prayer to its end when he sensed such an urgent need to piss that he knew he would befoul the bed he was lying on, the lovely coil-spring mattress, or even his lovely gray carpet, if he did not succeed in finding relief somewhere within the next few seconds. This brought him totally to himself. Groaning, he stood up, cast a desperate glance at the door—no, he could not walk through that door, even if the damned bird were gone now, he would no longer make it to the toilet— walked over to the basin, ripped open his bathrobe, ripped down his pajama bottoms, turned on the tap, and pissed into the basin.

He had never done anything like that before. The very thought was a horror, pissing into a lovely white, cleanly scrubbed washbasin intended for personal hygiene and dishwashing! Never would he have believed that he could sink so low, never that he might find himself physically constrained to commit such a sacrilege. But now, as he watched his piss flow, totally uninhibited and unchecked, blending with the water and gurgling down the drain, and as he felt the glorious easing of the pressure in his abdomen, tears flowed from his eyes at the same time for the very shame of it. When he was finished he let the water run for a while and gave the basin a thorough scrubbing with a scouring liquid, eliminating even the slightest traces of the outrage he had committed. "Once doesn't count," he muttered to himself as if apologizing to the washbasin, to the room, or to himself, "once doesn't count, it was a one-time emergency, it will certainly never happen again. . . ."

He grew calmer now. The activities of wiping up, storing away the bottle of scouring liquid, wringing out the rag—well-practiced, comforting dexterities—restored his sense of pragmatic action. He looked at the clock. It was just a little after seven fifteen. Normally by seven fifteen he would already have shaved and made his bed. But the delay was within acceptable limits; he would be able to make it up, if necessary by forgoing his breakfast. If he forwent breakfast—so he calculated—he would actually be seven minutes ahead of his regular schedule. The crucial thing was that he had to leave his room by five after eight at the latest, since he had to be at the bank by a quarter past eight. How he would manage that he did not know yet, but he still had forty-five minutes' grace. That was a lot. Forty-five minutes was a lot of time when you had just stared death in the eye and only narrowly escaped a heart attack. The time counted for double once you were no longer under the imperative pressure of a full bladder. His first decision therefore was to behave as if nothing had happened and to pursue his usual morning chores. He filled the washbasin with hot water and shaved.

While he was shaving, he engaged in painstaking deliberation. "Jonathan Noel," he said to himself, "you were a soldier in Indochina for two years and mastered many a risky situation there. If you ravel up all your courage and all your native wit, if you arm yourself accordingly and if you have good luck, then your sortie out of your room should be a success. But what if it does succeed? What if you indeed get by that ghastly animal at your door, make it to the stairway unscathed, and find yourself out of harm's way? You will go on to work, will be able to get through the day unbruised—but what do you do then? Where will you go this evening? Where will you spend the night?" Because having once escaped it, he did not want to meet the pigeon a second time; under no circumstances could he live under the same roof with this pigeon, not a single day, not a single night, not a single hour—that much was settled, unalterably settled. He would therefore have to be prepared to spend the night and perhaps the following nights in a boardinghouse. That meant that he had to take his shaving gear, toothbrush, and a change of underwear with him. Besides which he would need his checkbook and, just to be sure, his savings book as well. He had twelve hundred francs in his checking account. That would last for two weeks, assuming he found a cheap hotel. If the pigeon was then still blocking his room, he would have to dip into his savings. He had six thousand francs in his savings account, a lot of money. He could live in a hotel for months on that. And in addition he would still

be getting his salary, three thousand seven
hundred francs a month, take home. On the
other hand he had to pay Madame Lassalle
eight thousand francs at year's end, the last
installment for his room. For his room. For
this room that he would no longer be living
in. How was he to explain to Madame Lassalle
a request to postpone the last payment? He
could hardly say to her: "Madame, I cannot
pay you the last installment of eight thousand
francs, since I've been living in a hotel for
months now because the room that I intended
to buy from you is blockaded by a pigeon."
He could hardly say that, could he? . . . Then
it occurred to him that he still owned five gold
pieces, five napoleons, each of them easily
worth a good six hundred francs, which he had
bought for fear of inflation during the Al-
gerian war of 1958. By no means ought he to
forget to take along those five napoleons. . . .
And a slender golden bracelet that he still had
from his mother. And his transistor radio.
And an elegant silver-plated ballpoint that
each of the bank employees had received for

Christmas. If he were to sell all these treasures, he could, if he were utterly frugal, live in the hotel until the end of the year and still pay Madame Lassalle her eight thousand francs. After January 1, the prospects would look better, since he would then be the owner of the room and would no longer have to come up with the rent. And perhaps the pigeon would not survive the winter. How long did a pigeon live? Two years, three years, ten years? And what if it was an old pigeon? Perhaps it would die within the week? Perhaps it would die this very day. Perhaps it had come for the sole purpose of dying. . . .

Once he had finished shaving, he drained the basin, rinsed it, filled it again, washed his torso and feet, brushed his teeth, drained the basin yet again, and wiped it clean with a rag. Then he made his bed.

Under the cupboard stood an old cardboard suitcase where he kept his dirty clothes, which he carted off to the laundry once a month. He pulled it out, emptied it, and put it on his bed. It was the same suitcase with which he had traveled from Charenton to Cavaillon in 1942, the same one with which he had come to Paris in 1954. And now as he saw this old suitcase lying on his bed, and as he began to fill it, not with dirty but with clean clothes, with a pair of oxfords, with underwear, his iron, checkbook, and prized treasures—as if for a journey—the tears rose again to his eyes, this time, however, not from shame but from quiet desperation. It seemed to him as if he had been hurled back thirty years, as if he had lost thirty years of his life.

When the packing was completed, it was a quarter to eight. He dressed, first in his regular uniform: gray trousers, blue shirt, leather jacket, leather belt with a holster for his pistol, gray official cap. Then he armed himself for his encounter with the pigeon. Most of all he was disgusted by the thought that it could come into physical contact with him, peck at his ankle perhaps or, fluttering up, brush his hands or his neck with its wings, or even settle down on him with its clawlike feet splayed. And so he did not put on his lightweight oxfords, but his rough, high leather boots with the lamb's-wool inner soles, which he normally used only in January or February, slipped into his winter coat, buttoned it up from top to bottom, wrapped a wool scarf around his neck and up over his chin, and protected his hands with lined leather gloves. In his right hand he held an umbrella. At seven minutes to eight, thus equipped, he stood ready to dare the sortie from his room.

He took off his official cap and laid an ear to the door. Nothing was to be heard. He put the cap back on, settling it firmly on his brow, picked up the suitcase and placed it at the ready beside the door. In order to have his right hand free, he hung the umbrella over his wrist, grasped the knob with his right hand, the button on the security lock with his left, turned back the bolt, and opened the door a crack. He peered out.

The pigeon was no longer sitting at the door. On the tile where it had sat there was now an emerald green splotch about the size of a five-franc piece and a tiny white downy feather that trembled softly in the draft from the door crack. Jonathan shuddered with disgust. He would have loved to slam the door shut again. His instincts were to retreat, back into the safety of his room, away from the terror out there. But then he saw that it was not just a single splotch, but that there were many splotches. The whole section of hallway that he could survey was sprinkled with these emerald green, moistly shimmering splotches. But remarkably what happened was not that Jonathan's repulsion grew more intense, but that on the contrary, he felt a compulsion to resist: he would perhaps have retreated before that single splotch and that single feather and have closed the door, for good and all. Except that the pigeon's having apparently shat the entire hallway full—the pervasiveness of this loathsome phenomenon—mobilized his courage. He opened the door all the way.

Now he saw the pigeon. It was sitting to his right at a distance of about five feet, at the very end of the hall, crouched in one corner. So little light fell on the spot, and Jonathan cast such a brief glance in that direction, that he could not discern whether it was asleep or awake, whether its eye was open or closed. He did not want to know either. He would have preferred not to have seen it at all. In his book on tropical fauna he had once read that certain animals, above all orangutans, pounced on you only if you looked them in the eye; if you ignored them, then they left you alone. Perhaps that was true of pigeons as well. At any rate, Jonathan decided to act as if the pigeon were no longer present, or at least to look upon it no more.

Slowly he shoved his suitcase out into the hall, very slowly and carefully out between the green splotches. Then he opened the umbrella, held it with his left hand before chest and face like a shield, stepped into the hall, paying constant attention to the splotches on the floor, and pulled the door closed behind him. Despite all intentions to act as if nothing were happening, he took fright again nonetheless, and his heart pounded clear up into his throat, and when he could not immediately extract his key from his pocket with his gloved fingers, he began to tremble so from nervousness that he almost dropped the umbrella, and in grabbing for it with his right hand in order to clamp it between shoulder and cheek, his key actually did fall to the floor, just missing the splotch by a hair, and he had to bend down to pick it up, and once he finally had a firm hold on it, he was so excited it took three thrusts at the lock, each one a miss, before he finally got the key in and turned it over twice. In that moment it seemed to him as if he heard a fluttering behind him . . . or was it only his umbrella striking the wall? . . . But then he heard it again, unmistakable, a short, dry flap of wings, and he panicked. He snatched the key from the lock, snatched up his suitcase, and scurried off. The raised umbrella scraped along the wall, the suitcase bumped against the doors to the other rooms, in the middle of the hall the opened casements of the window were in his way—he forced past them, giving the umbrella such a violent and clumsy tug behind him that the taut material ended in tatters, to which he paid no attention; none of this was important, he just wanted to get out, out, out.

Only when he had reached the stairway landing did he stop for a moment to close the cumbersome umbrella and cast a glance back: The bright rays of the morning sun fell through the window, engraving a sharp-edged block of light out of the dusky shadows of the hallway. You could hardly see through it, and only when he squinted his eyes and strained to look, did Jonathan see how, way at the back, the pigeon extracted itself from the dark corner, took a few rapid, wobbling steps forward, and then settled back down again, right in front of the door to his room.

He turned away, his flesh creeping, and descended the stairs. In that moment he was certain that he would never be able to return.

With each stair tread he took, he grew calmer. At the third-floor landing, a sudden wave of heat triggered his awareness of the fact that he had on a winter coat, scarf, and fur-lined boots. Any moment a serving girl on her way out to shop could step through one of the doors leading from the kitchens of the elegant apartments onto these back stairs, or Monsieur Rigaud might set out his empty wine bottles, or worse still, Madame Lassalle herself, for whatever reason—she arose early, did Madame Lassalle, she was up even now, you could smell the penetrating odor of coffee up and down the staircase and Madame Lassalle would have the back door to her kitchen wide open, and there he, Jonathan, would stand before her on the stairs, in this grotesque winter costume in the brightest August sunlight—and he simply could not walk away from an embarrassment of such magnitude, he would have to explain himself, but how could he do that?, he would have to invent some lie, but what sort of lie? There was no plausible explanation for his appearance at the moment. People could only assume he was crazy. Perhaps he was crazy.

He set his suitcase down, extracted the pair of oxfords from it, and quickly took off gloves,

coat, scarf, and boots; slipped into the oxfords, stuffed scarf, gloves, and boots into
the suitcase, and threw the coat over his arm.
And now, so he thought, his existence was once
again justified in any man's eyes. If the need
arose, he could always maintain that he was
taking his wash to the laundry and his winter
coat to the cleaner's. With considerable relief,
he continued his descent.

In the back courtyard he met the concierge,
who with her little wagon was wheeling the
empty garbage cans in from the street. At once
he felt himself caught red-handed, his step
faltered. He could not pull back into the
darkness of the stairwell, she had already
seen him, he must go on. "Good day, Monsieur
Noel," she said as he passed her at an inten-
tionally vigorous pace.

"Good day, Madame Rocard," he muttered. They never said more than that to one
another. For ten years—as long as she had
lived in the building—he had never said more
to her than "Good day, madame," and "Good
evening, madame," and "Thank you, ma-

34

dame," when she handed him his mail. Not that he had anything against her. She was not an unpleasant person. She was no different from her predecessor and her predecessor's predecessor. Like all concierges, she was of an indefinable age, between late forties and late sixties; like all concierges, her gait was shuffling, her figure stoutish, her complexion maggoty, and her odor musty. When she was not carting the garbage cans in or out, cleaning the staircase, or hastily doing some shopping, she sat by fluorescent light in her little concierge's lodge at the passage between street and courtyard, let her television run, sewed, ironed, cooked, and got drunk on cheap red wine and vermouth, just as every other concierge did. No, he really had nothing against her. He just had something against concierges in general, because concierges were people who for professional reasons were constantly watching other people. And Madame Rocard in particular was someone who permanently watched him, Jonathan, in particular. It was completely impossible to pass by Madame

Rocard without her taking notice of you, even if it was only of the briefest sort, hardly a visible lifting of the eyes. Even when she was sitting asleep in her chair inside her lodge—which chiefly occurred in the early hours of afternoon and after her evening meal—the soft creak of the entrance door sufficed for her to awaken for a few seconds and to take notice of the passerby. No one in the world took notice of Jonathan as often and as precisely as Madame Rocard. He had no friends. At the bank he was, so to speak, part of the inventory. Customers regarded him as decor, not as a person. In the supermarket, on the street, on the bus (but when did he ever ride a bus!), his anonymity was preserved by the mass of others. The sole exception was Madame Rocard, who recognized and scrutinized him and paid him her candid attention at least twice daily. She was thus able to gain such intimate information about his modus vivendi as: what clothing he wore, how often per week he changed his shirt, whether he had washed his hair, what he brought home with him for his evening meal, if and from whom he received mail. And although, as noted, Jonathan had nothing against Madame Rocard personally and although he knew quite well that her indiscreet glances originated not from any curiosity but rather from her sense of professional duty, nonetheless he always felt those glances falling upon him like some mute reproach, and every time he walked past Madame Rocard—even after so many years—he felt a brief, hot surge of indignation: Why in the hell is she watching me again? Why is she checking me over yet again? Why, just for once, doesn't she allow me my integrity by taking no notice of me? Why are people so pushy?

And because, considering what had just happened, he was especially touchy today and bore, or so he believed, the misery of his existence for all to see in the form of a suitcase and a winter coat, Madame Rocard's glances struck him as especially painful, above all her greeting of "Good day, Monsieur Noel!" seemed to him the purest mockery.

The wave of outrage, which until now had been dammed up within him, crested into outright fury, and he did something he had never done: He stopped, once he had passed Madame Rocard, stood there, set his suitcase down, laid his winter coat over it, and turned around; turned around, fiercely resolved to counter the impertinence of both her glance and her greeting once and for all. He did not yet know what he would do or say as he walked toward her. He only knew *that* he would do and say something. The wave of his outrage had broken and bore him toward her, and his courage was boundless.

She had set the garbage cans back in place and was about to return to her concierge's lodge when he confronted her, more or less in the middle of the courtyard. They came to a halt about two feet apart. He had never seen her maggoty face from so close up. The skin of her puffy cheeks seemed of great delicacy, like old, fragile silk, and her eyes, brown eyes, when viewed from close up, had no meddlesome sting to them at all, revealing instead something soft, something almost like virginal modesty. But Jonathan did not allow the sight of such details—which certainly contradicted the image of Madame Rocard he bore within him—to bother him. Adding an official note to his demarche, he tapped his uniform cap and said rather caustically: "Madame! I must have a word with you." (At this point he still did not know what he actually wanted to say.)

"Yes, Monsieur Noel?" Madame Rocard said with a little twitch that tilted her head back.

She looks like a bird, Jonathan thought; like a little frightened bird. And he repeated his address in the same caustic voice: "Madame, I have the following to say to you . . ." only to join her in hearing, much to his own amazement, how the driving force of his outrage quite involuntarily took shape as: "There is a bird, madame, at the door to my room," and further, specifying, "a pigeon, madame. It is sitting on the tiles at my door." And only at this point did he succeed in reining in the gush of words coming from his subconscious and steering them in a particular direction with the addendum: "This pigeon, madame, has already soiled the entire hallway on the seventh floor with its droppings."

Madame Rocard shifted her weight a couple of times from one foot to the other, threw her head back a little further still, and said: "Where did the pigeon come from, monsieur?"

"I don't know," said Jonathan. "Probably it forced its way in through the hall window. The window is open. The window should always be kept closed. That's part of the house rules."

"Probably one of the students opened it," said Madame Rocard, "on account of the heat."

"That may be," said Jonathan. "But it should be kept closed nevertheless. Especially in summer. If a thunderstorm comes up, it can bang shut and get broken. That's what happened once, in the summer of 1962. At the time it cost one hundred fifty francs to replace the pane. Since then the house rules state that the window must always be kept closed."

He was indeed aware that there was something ridiculous about his constant reference to the house rules. Nor did it interest him in the least how the pigeon had got in. Indeed, he did not want to go into particulars about the pigeon; this horrible problem was no one's concern but his own. He wanted to give vent to his outrage at Madame Rocard's glances, nothing more, and that had been accomplished with those first sentences. The outrage had ebbed now. He did not know how to go on from here.

"Someone will simply have to chase the pigeon off again and close the window," Madame Rocard said. She said it as if that were the simplest matter in the world and as if everything would then be all right again. Jonathan kept silent. With one glance he had got himself trapped in the brown fundament of her eyes, he was in danger of sinking, as if into a soft, brown swamp, and had to close his

41

own eyes for a second to get out of it and to clear his throat to find his voice again.

"It's . . ." he began, clearing his throat yet again, "it's so bad that there's nothing but splotches. Nothing but green splotches. And feathers too. It's soiled the whole hallway. That's the main problem."

"Of course, monsieur," Madame Rocard said, "the hallway will have to be cleaned. But first, someone must chase off the pigeon."

"Yes," said Jonathan, "yes, yes . . ." and he thought: What's she thinking? What does she want? Why did she say: *someone* must chase off the pigeon? Does she perhaps mean that *I* should chase it off? And he wished that he had never dared accost Madame Rocard.

"Yes, yes," he stammered on, "someone . . . someone must chase it off. I . . . I would have chased it off long ago, but I didn't get around to it. I'm in a hurry. As you can see, I have my laundry with me today and my winter coat. I have to take the coat to be cleaned and the laundry to be washed, and then get to work. I'm in a great hurry, madame, which is why I couldn't chase off the pigeon. I simply wanted to report the incident to you. Especially because of the splotches. The main problem is that the pigeon has soiled the hallway with splotches and that's contrary to house rules. The house rules read that the hallway, stairs, and toilet are always to be kept clean."

He could not remember ever having carried on such a bungled conversation in all his life. His lies, it seemed to him, were apparent, crudely obvious, and the sole truth that they were meant to disguise—that he would never, ever be able to rout the pigeon, that indeed the pigeon had long since routed him—was most embarrassingly manifest; and even if Madame Rocard had not picked up on this truth from his words, she must certainly be able to read it now in his face, as he flushed and the blood rose to his head and his cheeks burned with shame.

Madame Rocard, however, acted as if she had noticed nothing (or perhaps she had really noticed nothing?) and just said: "Thank you for the information, monsieur. I'll take care of the matter when I get a chance," and, lowering her head, skirted around Jonathan to shuffle off to the outhouse beside her lodge and vanish inside it.

Jonathan watched her go. If he had had any hope whatever of someone's saving him from the pigeon, that hope vanished with the bleak vision of Madame Rocard vanishing into her outhouse. She's not going to take care of anything, he thought, of anything at all. And why should she? She's just a concierge and as such her job is to sweep the stairs and the hallway and to clean the shared toilet once a week, but not to rout pigeons. By this afternoon, at the latest, she'll be drunk on vermouth and have forgotten the entire affair, if she hasn't, at this very moment, forgotten it already. . . .

Jonathan was at the bank punctually at eight fifteen, exactly five minutes before the vice-president, Monsieur Vilman, and Madame Roques, the head cashier, arrived. Together they swung open the entrance doors: Jonathan the outer folding gate, Madame Roques the outer bulletproof glass door, Monsieur Vilman the inner bulletproof glass door. Then Jonathan and Monsieur Vilman used their socket keys to deactivate the alarm system; Jonathan and Madame Roques opened the double-locked fire door to the lower level; Madame Roques and Monsieur Vilman disappeared into the cellar to open the strong room with the appropriate keys, while Jonathan, having in the meantime locked his suitcase, umbrella, and winter coat in his locker next to the toilets, took his position at the inner bulletproof glass door and provided entry to the employees, arriving one by one, by pushing two buttons, which alternately released the inner and outer bulletproof glass doors electrically, like a series of sluice gates. By eight forty-five the whole staff had gathered, each of them having made his or her work station ready behind the counter, in the accounting room, or in the offices, and Jonathan left the bank to take up his position on the marble steps before the doorway. His real duties now began.

For thirty years now, from nine o'clock

in the morning until one in the afternoon and from two thirty in the afternoon until five thirty in the evening, these duties had consisted of nothing other than Jonathan's either standing stock-still at the doorway or at most patrolling back and forth in measured steps along the lowest three marble steps. Around nine thirty and between four thirty and five, there was a short break, occasioned by the arrival and subsequent departure of the black limousine of Monsieur Roedel, the president. That meant leaving his station on the marble steps, hurrying the twelve yards along the bank building to the entrance gate of the rear courtyard, shoving open the heavy steel grille, laying his hand to the rim of his cap in deferential greeting, and allowing the limousine to pass. Much the same sort of thing could happen early in the morning or late in the afternoon when the blue armored truck from Brink's Transport Service pulled up. The steel grille had to be opened for it as well, and its occupants likewise received a salute, not, to be sure, the deferential one with the palm placed

to the rim of his cap, but a more cursory salute
to colleagues, with the index finger at the rim
of his cap. Otherwise, nothing happened. Jonathan stood, stared, and waited. Sometimes he
stared at his feet, sometimes at the sidewalk,
sometimes he stared across to the café on the
other side of the street. Sometimes he wan-
dered along the lowest marble step, seven
paces to the left and seven paces to the right,
or he left the lowest step and took a position
on the second one, and sometimes, if the sun
was blazing down all too fiercely and the heat
was causing the water to squeeze against the
sweatband of his cap, he even scaled the third
step, which was shaded by the canopy of the
doorway, to stand there, once he had briefly
doffed his cap and wiped his moist brow
with his forearm, and to stare and wait.

He had once calculated that by the time of
his retirement he would have spent seventy-
five thousand hours standing on these three
marble steps. He would then assuredly be the
one person in all Paris—perhaps even in all
France—who had stood the longest time in

just one place. Presumably he had already achieved that, since by now he had spent fifty-five thousand hours on those marble steps. There were in fact very few permanently employed guards left in the city. Most banks subscribed to so-called tangible assets protection companies and let them place before their doors young, bowlegged, glumly self-absorbed fellows, who were soon replaced within a few months, often within weeks, by other, equally glumly self-absorbed fellows—ostensibly for reasons of work psychology: A guard's attention span, so it was said, diminishes if he serves too long at one and the same spot; his perception of events around him grows dull; he becomes lazy, careless, and thus unfit for his tasks. . . .

All nonsense! Jonathan knew better: A guard's attention was burnt out within hours. From the first day on, he was no longer consciously aware of his surroundings or even of the many hundreds of people who entered the bank—nor was that even necessary, for you could not distinguish a bank robber from a bank customer in any case. And even if a guard could do that and threw himself across the path of the robber, he would be shot down and dead long before he had so much as released the safety loop on his pistol holster, for robbers had an advantage over the guard that was impossible to equalize, that of surprise.

Like a sphinx, is how Jonathan thought of it (for he had once read about sphinxes in one of his books)—a guard was like a sphinx. He functioned not by some deed, but rather by his mere bodily presence. He confronted the potential robber with that and that alone. "You must pass by me," said the sphinx to the grave robber. "I cannot thwart you, but you must pass by me; and if you dare to do so, then the revenge of the gods and of the pharaoh's manes will come upon you!" And the guard: "You must pass by me, I cannot thwart you, but if you dare to do so, you will have to shoot me down, and the revenge of the courts will come upon you in the form of a conviction for murder!"

Now of course Jonathan knew quite well that the sphinx was in command of more effective sanctions than was a guard. No guard could threaten the revenge of the gods. And even if it was a robber who didn't give a hang about sanctions, the sphinx was hardly in danger. It was hewn from basalt, from purest rock, cast in bronze or built of solid brick. With no effort at all, it outlasted mere grave robbery by five thousand years . . . while during an attempted bank robbery, a guard would inevitably lose his life within five seconds. And yet they were alike, so Jonathan thought, the sphinx and the guard, for the power of both was not instrumental, it was symbolic. And solely in the awareness of this symbolic power—which was his pride and glory and the basis of his self-respect, which endowed him with his strength and stamina, which shielded him better than vigilance, weapons, or bullet-proof glass—Jonathan Noel had stood on the marble steps in front of the bank and held watch for thirty years now, without fear, without self-doubt, without the least sense of discontent and without the slightest look of glumness, until today.

But today everything was different. Today Jonathan was having no success whatever at achieving his sphinxlike calm. After only a few minutes he could feel the burden of his body as a painful pressure on his soles; he shifted his weight from one foot to the other and back again, sending him into a gentle stagger and making him interpolate little side-steps to keep his center of gravity—which until now he had always held on classical plumb—from slipping off balance. He also felt a sudden itch on his thigh, on the flank of his chest, and at the nape of his neck. After a while his forehead itched, as if it had become dry and chapped as it was sometimes in winter—whereas the day had in fact turned hot now, inexcusably hot really for nine fifteen in the morning; his brow was already as damp as it actually ought to have been around eleven . . . the itch moved to his arms, his chest, his back, down his legs; everywhere where there was skin he itched,

51

and he would have loved to scratch himself,
all abandon and voracity, but that just wasn't
done, ever, a guard scratching himself in
public! And so he took a deep breath,
thrust out his chest, hunched and relaxed his
back, raised and lowered his shoulders, em-
ploying such means to scrape against the inside of his clothing and provide relief. Such
extraordinary contortions and twitches, however, magnified the stagger again, and soon
the little sidestepping sallies no longer sufficed to maintain his balance, and Jonathan
found himself forced against custom to abandon his stance of a statuesque sentinel even
before the arrival of Monsieur Roedel's limousine at half past nine and to switch to patrolling back and forth, seven paces to the left,
seven paces to the right. In doing so, he tried
to clamp his gaze on the edge of the second
marble step, to let it move him back and
forth as a kind of trolley on a steady rail, so
that through the monotone infusion of just this
one image—the edge of the marble step—the
sphinxlike composure for which he longed

might arise within him and let him forget the heaviness of his body and his itchy skin and this whole curious turmoil of body and mind. But that did no good. The trolley was constantly derailing. Every time his eyelid batted, his gaze broke from the confounded edge and sprang to some other thing: to a scrap of newspaper on the sidewalk, to a foot in blue stockings, some woman's back, a shopping basket with loaves of bread in it, the knob on the outer bulletproof-glass door, the shining red rhombus of the Tabac monopoly above the café opposite, a bicycle, a straw hat, a face. . . . And nowhere did he succeed in getting a firm clamp on things, in establishing a new point of fixation that might support and orient him. Hardly was the straw hat on his right in focus, when a bus dragged his gaze down the street to his left, only to hand it over a few yards farther on to a white convertible sports car, which then drove it back along the street to the right, where in the meantime the straw hat had disappeared; his eye roamed frantically in the throng of pass-

ersby, in the throng of hats, got snagged on
a rose swaying on a totally different hat,
wrenched itself away, and finally fell back to
the edge of the step, but once again could
not rest there, strayed away, fidgeted from
point to point, from spot to spot, from line
to line. . . . It was as if the air were wavering
in the heat today, the way it does only on
the hottest July afternoons. Transparent veils
fluttered before things. The outlined contours
of buildings, eaves, rooftops were glittering
and garish, and at the same time indistinct,
frazzled. The edges of curbs and the cracks
between the stone squares of the sidewalk—
normally as if drawn with a straightedge—
meandered along in glistening curves. And
the women seemed all to be wearing garish
clothes today, they blazed past like flames,
drawing his gaze and yet not holding it fast.
Nothing was left clearly delineated. Nothing
was left to be precisely fixed. Everything
quivered.

It's my eyes, Jonathan thought. I've turned
nearsighted during the night. I need glasses.

As a child he had had to wear glasses at one point, not strong ones, minus 0.75 diopter, left and right. It was very strange that this nearsightedness was giving him trouble again now at his advanced age. With age you were more likely to get farsighted, he had read, and your old nearsightedness decreased. Maybe what he was suffering from was not classic nearsightedness at all, but something that could in fact no longer be cured by glasses: a cataract, glaucoma, a torn retina, cancer of the eye, a tumor in his brain pressing down on the optic nerve. . . .

He was so very busy with this dreadful thought that the repeated short honks failed to force their way into his conscious mind. Only with the fourth or fifth one—someone was honking in drawn-out tones now—did he hear and react and lift his head: And there indeed at the entrance grille stood Monsieur Roedel's black limousine! They honked again and even waved, as if they had been waiting for several minutes now. At the entrance grille! Monsieur Roedel's limousine! When had he ever missed its approach? He normally did not even have to look, he sensed that it was coming, he could hear it in the hum of the motor, he could have been asleep and would have awakened like a dog at the approach of Monsieur Roedel's limousine.

He did not rush, he plunged toward it— almost falling in his haste—he unlocked the grille, pushed it back, he saluted, let them pass, he could feel his heart pounding and his hand trembling against the rim of his cap.

When he had closed the gateway and returned to the main entrance, he was bathed in sweat. "You missed Monsieur Roedel's limousine," he muttered to himself in a voice quivering with despair and repeated it as if he could not grasp it himself: "You missed Monsieur Roedel's limousine . . . you missed it, you've failed, you have flagrantly neglected your duties, you're not just blind, you're deaf, you're old and worn out, you're no longer fit to be a guard."

He had arrived at the lowest of the marble steps; he stepped up on it and tried to stand at attention again. He noticed at once that he was not succeeding. His shoulders wouldn't go square anymore, his arms dangled at his trouser seams. He knew what a ridiculous figure he made at that moment, and could do nothing about it. In his despair he looked at the sidewalk, at the street, at the café opposite. The shimmering in the air had ceased. Things stood on the plumb again, the lines ran straight, the world lay clear before his eyes. He heard the noise of the traffic, the hiss of the bus doors, the shouts of the waiters from the café, the clattering of the women's high-heeled shoes. Neither his vision nor his hearing was in the least affected. But sweat was running in streams from his brow. He felt weak. He turned around, climbed the second step, climbed the third step, and took up position in the shade of the column beside the outer doors of bulletproof glass. He crossed his hands behind his back so that they were touching the column. Then he let himself fall gently back, against his own hands and against the column, and leaned, for the first time in his thirty-year career of service. And for a few seconds he closed his eyes. He was so very ashamed of himself.

During the noon break, he fetched his suitcase, coat, and umbrella from the locker and walked up the nearby rue Saint-Placide, where he found a small hotel inhabited primarily by students and foreign workers. He demanded their cheapest room, they offered him one for fifty-five francs, he took it sight unseen, paid in advance, left his baggage at the reception desk. At a kiosk he bought himself two raisin rolls and a pint of milk and walked over to the place Boucicaut, a small park in front of the Bon Marché department store. He sat down on a bench in the shade and ate.

Two benches away squatted a clochard. The clochard had a bottle of white wine between his thighs, half a baguette in his hand, and a bag of smoked sardines lying next to him on the bench. He pulled the sardines out of the bag by the tail, one after the other, bit each head off, spat it out, and stuck the rest

58

in his mouth. Then a piece of bread, a large swallow from the bottle, and a moan of content. Jonathan knew the man. In winter he always sat on the grate near the delivery entrance of the department store, just above the cellar where the furnace was, and in summer in front of the boutiques on the rue de Sèvres or at the door of the traveler's aid or next to the post office. He had lived in the neighborhood for decades, about as long as Jonathan had. And Jonathan remembered that when he had first seen him back then, thirty years ago, a kind of angry envy had risen up in him, envy of the happy-go-lucky way the man led his life. While Jonathan fell in for duty every day at nine on the dot, the clochard would come along at ten or eleven; and while Jonathan had to stand at attention, the fellow would lounge comfortably on a cardboard box and have a smoke; while Jonathan guarded the bank hour after hour, day after day, and year after year, at the risk of his life and as a way of painfully earning his keep, the fellow did nothing but trust in the sympathy and assistance of his fellow men, who tossed their cash into his cap. And he never seemed to be in a bad mood, not even when his cap remained empty, never seemed to suffer or to be afraid or even bored. He always exuded an infuriating self-assurance and self-satisfaction, an exasperating, publicly displayed aura of freedom.

But then, once, in the mid-sixties, in autumn, as Jonathan was walking into the rue Dupin post office and at the entrance almost stumbled over a wine bottle placed atop a cardboard box between a plastic bag and the familiar cap with a few coins in it, and as he stopped automatically for a moment to look for the clochard, not because he missed him as a person but because the focal point of this still life of bottle, bag, and box was absent, he spotted him on the far side of the street, squatting between two parked cars, and watched as the man relieved himself: He was crouching beside the curb with his trousers pulled down to his knees, his rear turned toward Jonathan, totally exposed. People were passing by, anyone could see it: a pasty white rear end brindled with blue smudges and reddish scabby spots, that looked like the rear end of a bedridden old man—whereas the man was in fact no older than Jonathan himself at the time, thirty perhaps, at most thirty-five years old. And from this scruffy rear end a jet of brown, soupy liquid, of monstrous force and quantity, spurted onto the pavement to form a puddle, a pond, that sloshed about his shoes, and the splash was flung high and low over his soiled socks, thighs, trousers, shirt, everything. . . .

So wretched, so nauseating, so ghastly was the sight, that even now the mere memory made Jonathan shudder. At the time, after staring in horror for a moment, he had fled into the post office, paid his electric bill, then, though he really did not need them, bought some stamps to prolong his stay in the post office till he could be sure that on leaving he would not meet the clochard doing his business. When he did leave, he squinted, lowered his gaze and forced himself not to glance to the far side of the street, but hard to the left, up the rue Dupin, and he walked that way as well, to his left, although he certainly had no business to attend to there, simply so that he would not have to pass the spot with the wine bottle, the box, and the cap, willingly made a wide detour, via the rue du Cherche-Midi and the boulevard Raspail, before reaching the rue de la Planche and the haven of his room.

From that hour on, Jonathan's soul was dead to every sense of envy for the clochard. If, until then, a gentle doubt had still stirred within him from time to time about whether there was any meaning in a man's spending one-third of his life standing at the entrance of a bank, while occasionally opening a grille and saluting for the president's limousine, always the same, with minimal vacation and minimal pay, of which the greatest part disappeared in the form of taxes, rent, and social security payments . . . whether there was any meaning in all of this, the answer now appeared with the clarity of that horrible vision on the rue Dupin: Yes, there was meaning. It was indeed very meaningful, for it safe-guarded him from baring his rear end in public and shitting in the street. What could be more miserable than having to bare your rear end in public and shit in the street? What could be more demeaning than those pulled-down trousers, that crouch, that coerced ugly nakedness? What could be more wretched and humbling than being forced to do your em-barrassing business before the eyes of the world? Nature's necessity! The very term be-trayed its tormented victim. And like anything that you had to do out of duress, it demanded, for it to be at all bearable, the radical absence of other people . . . or at least the appearance of their absence: a wood if you found your-self in the country; a bush if you were over-come in an open field, or at least a farmer's furrow, or twilight or, if there was nothing else, a good steep bank that commanded a view of several miles in all directions, with no one in sight. And in the city? With its teem-ing masses? Where it was never really dark? Where even the ruins of an abandoned lot offered no adequate safeguard against obtrusive stares? In the city, nothing but a good lock and bolt helped you distance yourself from other people. And the man who did not have this one, this sure refuge for the necessity of nature, was the most miserable and pitiable of men, and freedom just silly talk. Jonathan could have managed on very little money. He could imagine himself wearing a shabby jacket, tattered trousers. If need be, and if all his romantic imagination were mobilized, it would even have seemed conceivable for him to sleep on a cardboard box and to reduce the intimacy of his own home to some nook, a heating grate, a stairwell in a subway station. But if you could not close a door behind you to take a shit in the city— even if it was just the door to a shared toilet— if this one, most essential freedom was taken from you, the freedom, that is, to withdraw from other people when necessity called, then all other freedoms were worthless. Then life had no more meaning. Then it would be better to be dead.

Once Jonathan had come to the realization that the essence of human freedom consisted in the possession of a shared toilet and that this essential freedom was at his disposal, he was immediately seized with a profound satisfaction. Yes, it was indeed right to have arranged his life as he had! He led a thoroughly successful existence. There was nothing, absolutely nothing whatever to regret or to envy other people for.

From that hour on, he stood on sturdier legs, as it were, before the entrance of the bank. There he stood as if cast in bronze. The solid self-satisfaction and self-assurance, which until then he had attributed to the person of the clochard, had flowed into him like molten metal, had hardened to an inner suit of armor, had given him specific gravity. Henceforth nothing could shake him and no doubt could cause him to waver. He had found his way to sphinxlike imperturbability. For the clochard—whenever he met him or saw him sitting somewhere—he felt only the sentiment that is generally termed tolerance: a very lukewarm emotional stew of disgust, contempt, and sympathy. The man no longer ruffled him. The fellow was of no consequence to him.

He had been of no consequence to him until this very day as Jonathan sat in the place Boucicaut consuming his raisin rolls and drinking milk from a paper carton. Normally he would have gone home during the midday break. After all, he lived only five minutes away. Normally he would have fixed himself something warm on his hot plate at home, an omelet, fried eggs and ham, noodles and grated cheese, soup left over from the day before and a salad and a cup of coffee. It had been an eternity since he had sat on a park bench at midday and eaten raisin rolls and drunk milk from a carton. Actually he had no special liking for sweets. Nor for milk either. But he had paid out fifty-five francs for the hotel room today; it would have seemed an extravagance to him to have gone to a café and there ordered an omelet, salad, and beer.

The clochard on the bench across the way had finished his meal. After the sardines and the bread, he had dined on cheese, pears, and cookies as well, taken a big pull on his wine bottle, given a sigh of deep contentment, and rolled his jacket into a pillow, bedding his head on it, stretching his lazy, satiated body out on the bench for a noontime nap. Now he slept. Sparrows came hopping over to peck away at the bread crumbs, then, attracted by the sparrows, pigeons waddled their way to the bench to hack with their black beaks at the sardine heads that had been bitten off. The clochard did not let the birds disturb him. He slept soundly and peacefully.

Jonathan watched him. And as he watched him, a strange disquiet came over him. This disquiet was not fed by envy as in the old days, but by amazement: How was it possible—he asked himself—that this man, well over fifty by now, was still alive at all? Given his thoroughly irresponsible way of life, should he not long ago have starved or frozen to death, been cut down by cirrhosis of the liver—be dead at any rate? Instead, he ate and drank with the best of appetites, slept the sleep of the just and, wearing a cotton jacket and patched trousers—which of course had long ago replaced those that he had pulled down on the rue Dupin, relatively smart, almost fashionable corduroy trousers, apart from a repair here and there—gave the impression of a firmly grounded personality in finest harmony with the world and enjoying life . . . whereas he, Jonathan—and his amazement gradually mounted to a kind of nervous bewilderment—whereas he, who his whole life long had been a well-behaved and orderly fellow, unpretentious, almost ascetic, clean, always punctual and obedient, reliable, respectable . . . and every sou he had he had earned himself, and always paid cash, for his utility bill, his rent, the concierge's Christmas tip . . . and never incurred debts, never been a burden to anyone, never once been sick or cost social service agencies a centime . . . never done anything to hurt anyone, had never, ever wanted anything from life except to maintain and guarantee his own modest, small contentment of soul . . . whereas he now saw himself, at age fifty-three, plunging head over heels into a crisis that confounded the life's plan he had devised for himself and was making him crazy and confused and had him eating raisin rolls for the pure confusion of it, and for fright. Yes, he was frightened! God knows, he needed only to look at this sleeping clochard and he started trembling with fright: All at once he was dreadfully frightened that he might have to become like the dissipated man there on the bench. How quickly it could happen, impoverished and on the skids! How quickly the apparently solidly laid foundation of one's existence could crumble. You missed Monsieur Roedel's limousine, came flashing through his mind again. Something that never happened before and that never ought to have happened, happened today nonetheless: You missed the limousine, and tomorrow perhaps you'll miss work entirely, or lose the key to the steel gate, and next month you'll be ignominiously fired, and you won't find a new job, because who would hire a failure? No one can live on unemployment checks, by then you will have long since lost your room—there's a pigeon living in it, a family of pigeons lives there, fouling and ravaging your room—the hotel bills grow to incalculable sums, in your worry you start drinking, drink more and more, drink away every centime you've saved, become a slave to booze with no way out, get sick, ridden by decay, lice, depravity, are driven out of your final flophouse, you haven't a sou left, you stand before total ruin, out on the street, you sleep, you live in the street, you shit in the street, you're at the end of your tether, Jonathan, within a year you'll be at the end, like that clochard in his rags on the park bench, you'll be lying there, his brother in degradation.

His mouth had become dry. He turned his gaze from the *mene tekel* of the sleeping man and choked down the last bites of his raisin roll. It took an eternity before the bite got to his stomach, it crept down his esophagus with snail-like slowness, sometimes almost sticking there and pressing and hurting as if a nail were being driven into his chest, till Jonathan thought he would choke to death on this nauseating mouthful. But then the thing did slide on, one tiny piece and then another tiny piece, and finally it was down, and the cramping pain subsided. Jonathan took a deep breath. He would leave now. He didn't want to stay here any longer, although the midday break would not be over for a half hour yet. He had had enough. The place was spoiled for him. With the back of his hand he swept his lap and uniform trousers clean of the few raisin roll crumbs that, despite all the care he had taken, had fallen as he ate, pinched the folds of his creases, got up and walked away, without casting one glance more at the clochard.

He was already back on the rue de Sèvres when it occurred to him that he had left the empty milk carton on the park bench, and that troubled him, for he hated it when other people left their trash lying on benches or simply tossed it on the street instead of where trash belonged, which was in the litter baskets set out everywhere. He himself had never simply tossed trash away or let it lie on a park bench, never, not even out of negligence or forgetfulness, something like that simply did not happen to him . . . and therefore he did not want it to happen to him today, especially not today, not on this precarious day on which so much damage had already been done. He was already on shaky ground as it was, was behaving like a fool as it was, like some irresponsible tramp, almost like a derelict—he had missed Monsieur Roedel's limousine! Had eaten raisin rolls for lunch in the park! If he were not careful, especially in little things, and did not put all his energy into stemming the tide of such apparently trivial matters, like leaving his milk carton behind, then he would soon lose his grip entirely, and nothing would prevent his ending in misery.

He therefore turned around and went back to the park. Even from a distance he could see that the bench on which he had sat was still vacant, and as he came nearer, to his relief he spotted the white carton of the milk container through the dark green of the bench's back slats. Apparently no one had noticed his carelessness, he could eradicate the unforgivable mistake. Stepping up to the bench from behind, he bent down, way over the back, grabbed the milk carton with his left hand, and in straightening up again, gave his body a decisive twist to the right, in about the same direction he knew the nearest litter basket to stand—and suddenly he felt his trousers being given an abrupt, violent, downward tug, and, since it had happened so suddenly and because he was in the midst of an upward rotating motion in exactly the opposite direction, he could not move with the tug. And at the same time there was an ugly noise, a loud *rip*, and across the skin of his left thigh, he felt the stroke of a draft that bespoke an unchecked invasion of air from the outside. For a moment he was so horrified that he dared not look. It also seemed to him that the *rip*—it was still echoing in his ears—had been so monstrously loud that more than his trousers had been torn, that the tear had ripped right through him, through the bench, through the whole park, like a gaping crevasse during an earthquake, and it seemed as if all the people roundabout

73

must have heard it, this terrible *rip*, and in their shock were now watching him, Jonathan, as its instigator. But no one was watching. The old women went on knitting, the old men went on reading their newspapers, the few children over on the playground went on sliding down the slide, and the clochard slept. Slowly Jonathan lowered his eyes. The tear was about five inches long. It ran from the lower corner of his left trouser pocket, which had caught, just as he rotated, on a screw protruding from the bench, then down his thigh, and not in an orderly fashion down the seam, but right through the middle of the lovely gabardine of his uniform, and then finally made a right angle, about two thumbs wide, with the crease, so that there was not simply a discreet rent in the material, but a glaring hole above which fluttered a triangular banner.

Jonathan felt adrenaline shooting into his bloodstream, the tingling stuff he had once read about—how in moments of great bodily danger and mental distress a gland of the kidneys poured it out to mobilize the body's last reserves for flight or for a battle to the death. In point of fact, it seemed to him as if he had been wounded, as if the gaping hole was not just in his trousers, but in his own flesh, a wound five inches long from which his blood, his very life, was gushing instead of circulating in its internal, closed system, and that he would die of this wound if he did not close it at once. But then there was the adrenaline, and even though he sensed that he was bleeding to death, its rush invigorated him most wondrously. His heart beat strong, his courage was great, his mind was suddenly quite clear and directed toward a single goal: "You have to do something at once," he shouted silently, "you must take action right now to close up this hole or you are lost!" And even as he asked himself what action he could take, he knew the answer—so rapid was the effect of the adrenaline, that splendid drug, such were the wings that fear lent to intelligence and resolve. Quick to decide, he snatched the milk carton, still in his left hand, with his right, crumpled it up, threw it away, somewhere, anywhere, on the grass, on the sandy path—he paid no attention. He pressed his free left hand to the hole at his thigh, and stumbled away—keeping his left leg as stiff as possible so that his hand would not slip, flailing wildly with his right arm—in a storm-tossed limping hobble, ran out of the park and up the rue de Sèvres; he had less than a half hour's time.

In the grocery department of the Bon Marché, at the corner of the rue du Bac, there was a seamstress. He had noticed her only a few days before. She sat way to the front, near the entrance, where the shopping carts were parked. She had a sign hanging at her sewing machine, and he could remember exactly how it read: JEANNINE TOPELL— ALTERATIONS AND REPAIRS—FAULTLESS AND FAST. This woman would help him. She had to help him—that is, if she wasn't on her lunch break herself at the moment. But she wouldn't be taking her lunch break, no, no, that would be too much bad luck. He couldn't have that much bad luck on one day. Not now. Not when his need was so great. When you were in direst need was when you had good luck, when you found help. Madame Topell would be at her spot and would help.

Madame Topell *was* at her spot! From the entrance to the grocery department he could already see her sitting at her machine and sewing. Yes, you could depend on Madame Topell, she even worked during her lunch break, faultless and fast. He ran to her, took up position next to the sewing machine, removed his hand from his thigh, cast a quick glance at his wristwatch—it was five after two—cleared his throat: "Madame!" he began.

Madame Topell finished the pleat of a red skirt she was working on, turned off the machine, and released the needle to free the cloth and cut the thread. Then she lifted her head and looked at Jonathan. She was wearing a very large pair of glasses with heavy, mother-of-pearl frames and thick convex lenses that made her eyes giant-sized and turned the sockets into deep, shaded pools. Her hair was chestnut in color and fell smoothly just over her shoulders and her lips were painted silvery violet. She was in her late forties perhaps, or maybe mid-fifties, she had the allure of women who can tell your fortune from cards or a crystal ball, the allure of a lady rather come down in the world, one whom the term "lady" no longer quite fits and to whom one nevertheless responds with instant trust. And even her fingers—she used her fingers to shove her glasses up on her nose a little to get a better look at Jonathan—even her fingers— stubby, sausagey and yet, despite all the hand- work, well-kept fingers with nails polished a silvery violet—had a semi-elegance that in- spired trust. "May I help you?" Madame Topell said in a slightly raspy voice.

Jonathan turned sideways to her, pointed at the hole in his trousers, and asked: "Can you mend that?" And because it seemed to him that he had formed the question too gruffly and might have betrayed his adrenaline- activated excitement, he added in a milder tone, as casually as possible: "It's a hole, a

little tear . . . a stupid bit of bad luck, madame. Can something be done about it, do
you think?"

Madame Topell let the glance of her giant
eyes wander down Jonathan to find the hole
at his thigh and bent forward to inspect it.
As she did, the smooth surface of her chestnut
hair divided from her shoulders up to the
back of her head and bared a short, white neck
padded with fat; and at the same time a
fragrance rose up from her, so heavy and
powdery and stupefying that Jonathan automatically threw back his head and sent his
gaze leaping from the nearby neck to the far
reaches of the supermarket; and for a moment
he saw before him the space in its totality,
with all its shelves and refrigerated cases and
stands for cheese and charcuterie and tables
for specials and pyramids of bottles and moun-
tains of vegetables and in the midst of it all,
the customers, hurrying about, shoving shopping carts, tugging tots behind them, and the
personnel, the stockers, the cashiers—a swarm-
ing, noisy crowd of people, at whose edge,

and exposed to whose every eye, stood Jonathan with his tattered trousers. . . . And the thought twitched across his brain that perhaps Monsieur Vilman, Madame Roques, or even Monsieur Roedel might be among the crowd and be observing him, Jonathan, while an equivocal portion of his body was being examined by a somewhat disreputable lady with chestnut hair. And he even grew a little queasy, especially since he could feel, good God, one of Madame Topell's sausagey fingers on the skin of his thigh flipping the torn banner of cloth back and forth. . . .

But then Madame reemerged from the depths of his thighs, leaned back in her chair, and the direct current from her perfume was interrupted, so that Jonathan could lower his head and remove his glance from the bewildering expanse of the room and turn his gaze to the propinquity of Madame Topell's large, convex lenses.

"Well?" he asked, and then again: "Well?" with a kind of alarmed urgency, as if he were a patient standing before his doctor and in fear of a devastating diagnosis.

"No problem," said Madame Topell. "We just have to lay something under it. And a little seam will show. Can't be done any other way."

"But that makes no difference at all," Jonathan said, "a little seam makes no difference at all, who would ever look at such an obscure spot?" And he glanced at his watch; it was fourteen after. "So you can take care of it? You can help me, madame?"

"Yes, of course," said Madame Topell, and shoved her glasses, which had slipped down somewhat during the examination of the hole, back up on her nose.

"Oh, thank you, madame," Jonathan said, "thank you very much. You've saved me from great embarrassment. And now I have another request: Could you . . . would you be so kind—I'm in a hurry you see, I have only"— and he looked at his watch again—"only ten minutes left—could you do it right away? I mean: here, now? Without delay?"

There are questions that are gainsaid simply in the asking. And there are requests whose total pointlessness becomes apparent

81

once one utters them and gazes into the eyes of the other person. Jonathan gazed into the shadowy giant eyes of Madame Topell and knew at once that it was all pointless, all purposeless, hopeless. He had known it already even as he asked his fidgety question, had known it, had felt it palpably in his body as the adrenaline level in his blood fell the moment he had looked at his watch: ten minutes! He felt as if he were falling himself, like someone standing on a fragile ice floe that is about to merge with the water. Ten minutes! How could anyone be in a position to plug this dreadful hole in ten minutes? It would never work. It simply couldn't work. After all, you couldn't mend the hole right there on his thigh. Something had to be laid under it and that meant taking off the trousers. But in the meantime, where would he find another pair, in the middle of the grocery department of the Bon Marché? Take off his own trousers and stand there in his underwear . . . ? Pointless, totally pointless.

"Right now?" Madame Topell asked, and

Jonathan, although he knew that it was all pointless, and although the abyss of defeat had engulfed him, nodded.

Madame Topell smiled. "Take a look, monsieur: Everything you see here"—and she pointed to a clothes rod two yards long, hung and piled full of dresses, jackets, trousers, blouses—"has to be done right now. I work ten hours a day."

"Yes, of course," Jonathan said, "I understand completely, madame, it was only a stupid question. How long do you think it will be before you can have my rip mended?"

Madame Topell turned back to her machine, tugged the material of the red skirt into place, and let the needle down. "If you bring me the trousers next Monday, they'll be ready in three weeks."

"In three weeks?" Jonathan repeated as if dazed.

"Yes," Madame Topell said, "in three weeks. Can't be done sooner."

And then she turned her machine on, and the needle hummed away, and at the same moment Jonathan felt as if he were no longer present. Of course he still could see Madame Topell sitting at her sewing machine table, barely an arm's length away, could see the chestnut head with the mother-of-pearl glasses, could see the thick fingers going speedily about their business and the whizzing needle pricking stitches in the hem of the red skirt . . . and he could also still see the blurred bustle of the supermarket in the background . . . but he suddenly no longer saw himself—that is, he no longer saw himself as a part of the world surrounding him. It was, rather, as if for a few seconds he were standing far away, outside of it, and were regarding this world through the wrong end of a telescope. And once again, just like this morning, he grew dizzy and he lurched. He took a step to one side and turned away and made for the exit. By moving, by walking, he found himself back in the world, the telescope effect vanished before his eyes. But inside him, the lurching went on. In the stationery department he bought a roll of Scotch tape. He used it to tape over the rent in his trousers, so that the triangular banner could no longer flop open with every step. Then he went back to work.

He spent the afternoon in a mood of anguish and anger. He stood in front of the bank, on the top step, directly in front of the column but not leaning against it, for he did not want to yield to his weakness. He couldn't have done so in any case, for in order to lean back without being noticed he would have had to cross both hands behind his back, and that was impossible, because he had to leave his left hand hanging down to cover the taped spot on his thigh. Instead, to make sure he kept his footing, he was forced to set his legs in the straddle position he hated, just as those stupid young fellows did it, and he noticed how that caused his spine to arch out and his neck, normally held so free and erect, to sink down between his shoulders, and with it his head and cap, and how that automatically caused him to look out from under the rim of his cap with the same glowering, stealthy gaze

and the same sulky air he found so very de-
spicable among the other guards. It was like
being crippled, a caricature of a guard, a
cartoon of himself. He despised himself. He
hated himself during these hours. His raging
self-hatred made him want to jump out of his
own skin, yes, he would literally have liked
to jump out of his skin, for the skin over his
whole body was itching now, and he could no
longer rub against his clothes because his skin
was sweating at every pore and his clothes
stuck to him like a second skin. And there,
where it didn't stick, where a little air remained between skin and clothing: on his
calves, on his forearms, in the furrow above
his breastbone . . . right there in that furrow
where the itch was really unbearable, because
the sweat was rolling down in great, wriggly
drops—that was precisely where he did *not*
want to scratch, no, he did not want to provide
himself with some practicable relief, for it
would not have changed his state of great and
general misery, but only have let it emerge
with greater clarity and ridiculousness. He

wanted to suffer now. The more he suffered, the better. The suffering suited him fine, it justified and inflamed his hate and his rage, and the rage and the hate in turn inflamed the suffering, for it set his blood surging ever more fiercely, continually squeezing new ripples of sweat from the pores of his skin. His face was sopping wet, the water dripped from his chin and the hair on his neck, and the band of his uniform cap cut into his sodden brow. But he would not have taken that cap off for anything in the world, not even for one brief moment. It was meant to sit screwed onto his head like a lid on a pressure cooker, to tighten around his temples like an iron ring, even if his head should burst. He wanted to do nothing to ease his misery. He stood there totally motionless, hour after hour. He noticed only how his spine was growing more and more twisted, how his shoulders, neck, and head sagged lower and lower, how his body assumed a posture that was increasingly squat and toadlike.

And finally—he was neither able nor willing to prevent it—the self-loathing dammed up inside him spilled over and gushed out, gushed out of glaring eyes that grew ever grimmer, angrier, beneath the brim of his cap, flooding the outside world as perfect, vulgar hate. Whatever came within his field of vision Jonathan coated with the vile patina of his hate. Indeed one could say that a real image of the world no longer passed the retina to enter the brain, but rather, in a reversal of the flow of light, that his eyes hurled warped internal images into the outside world: the waiters, for instance, across the way, on the other side of the street, on the sidewalk in front of the café, those good-for-nothing young, stupid waiters, who loitered among the tables and chairs, the louts, babbling and grinning and smirking and getting in the way of pedestrians and whistling after the girls, cock of the walk, and doing nothing except occasion-ally relaying a shouted order by bellowing it through the open doors to the bar: "A coffee! A beer! A lemon-lime soda!" and then finally easing themselves inside to juggle the order back out with feigned haste and serve it amid pretentious, pseudo-artistic waiterly gestures: the cup twirled down onto the table in a spiral, the Coke bottle clamped between the thighs and opened with a flick of the wrist, the check—held between the lips—spat first into one hand and then shoved under the ashtray while the other hand was already making change at the next table and scooping up piles of money, astronomical prices: five francs for an espresso, eleven francs for a short beer plus a surcharge of fifteen percent for the foppish service, and an extra tip to boot; yes, they expected that as well, fancy goldbrickers, dandies, an extra tip!—otherwise not so much as a "thanks" would pass their lips, not to mention a "good-bye"; without that extra tip, customers were simply thin air from then on and as they left the place saw nothing but arrogant waiters' backs and arrogant waiters' asses, above which the black overstuffed waiters' change purses were crammed into waistbands, for they considered that chic and nonchalant, the stupid nancies, putting their change purses on display like fat tushes—oh, he could have bayoneted, just with a look, these smug bastards in their loose, cool, short-sleeved waiters' shirts! He would have loved to run over and drag them out by the ear from under their shady awning and slap them right out on the street, give them a left, a right, a left, a right, whap smack, behind the ears, and tan their butts. . . .

But not just them! No, not just these snot-nosed waiters, but their customers, too, needed their butts tanned, the doltish pack of tourists, flitting about dressed in summer blouses and straw hats and sunglasses, guzzling overpriced drinks to refresh themselves, while other people earned a living by the sweat of their brow, standing. And then the drivers! Stupid monkeys in their stinking tin crates, fouling the air, setting up a hideous racket, with nothing better to do their whole life long than race up and down the rue de Sèvres. Doesn't it stink badly enough already? Isn't the street, the whole city, filled with racket enough? Doesn't the blazing heat from up there make things hot enough? Do you have to use the last bit of breathable air, suck it into your motors and burn it up and blow it back, mixed with poison and soot and hot fumes, into the noses of respectable citizens? Filthy pigs! Hooligans! They ought to wipe you out. Yes, they should! Flog you to death and get rid of you. Shoot you down. Every single one of you and all at one time. Oh! He had a mighty urge to pull out his pistol and let loose in every direction, right into the coffeehouse, smack through its glass windows, till there was nothing but crashing and tinkling, right into the middle of the ruck of cars or simply into the middle of one of the gigantic buildings across the way, those ugly, tall, menacing buildings, or into the air, straight up, into the heavens, yes into the hot sky, into the horrible, oppressive, vaporous, pigeon blue-gray sky, bursting it, sending the leaden lid crashing with one shot, smashing down and pulverizing everything and burying it all, all of it, the whole miserable, dreary, loud, stinking world: So universal, so titanic was Jonathan Noel's hate that after-

noon, that he would have liked to reduce the
world to rubble and ashes, because he had a
hole in his trousers!

But he didn't do it, thank God, he didn't
do it. He did not shoot at the heavens or at
the café opposite or at the passing cars. He
stood there, sweating and not making a move.
For the same force that had caused the raging
chimera to well up inside him, to go hurtling
out at the world in his gaze, paralyzed him so
totally that he could not move a muscle, let
alone put his hand to his weapon or crimp his
finger on the trigger, indeed, to the point where
he was no longer capable of simply shaking
his head to dislodge a small, tormenting drop
of sweat from the tip of his nose. The force
turned him to stone. Indeed, over these long
hours it had transformed him into the menacing, impotent form of a sphinx. It was something like the electrical tension that magnetizes
a lump of iron and holds it suspended, or the
powerful strength in the vault of an edifice
that grips each individual stone firmly in its
spell. It was subjunctive. Its whole potential

rested in "I would, I could, most of all I'd like to," and as he formulated these horrible subjunctive threats and curses in his mind, Jonathan also knew very well that he would never act on them. He was not the man for that. He was not a man to run amok, to commit a crime by reason of insanity or anguish of soul or spontaneous hatred; and not because for him such a crime would have seemed a moral abomination, but for the simple reason that he was totally incapable of *asserting* himself in either word or deed. He was not a man of action. He was a man of resignation.

By five o'clock in the evening, he found himself in such a desolate state that he thought he would never be able to leave his position at the column on the third step to the entrance of the bank and would die there. He felt he had aged at least twenty years and shrunk eight inches during the long hours under the brunt of the sun's heat and had been melted or crumbled by his internal rage, yes, it was like being crumbled, for he no longer felt the damp of his sweat, crumbled and weather-battered, combusted and shattered like a stony sphinx after five thousand years, and it would not be long now before he was totally desiccated and burnt up and shrunk to nothing and crumbled to nothing and decomposed to dust or ashes, and he would lie here on this spot, where he was only barely, painfully managing to keep on his feet, as a tiny little heap of dirt, until at last a breeze blew him away or a cleaning woman swept him away or the rain washed him away. Yes, that's how he would end: not as a respectable old gentleman living off his pension, at home in his own bed in his own four walls, but here at the entrance of the bank as a little pile of dirt. And he could only wish that it was already happening, that the process of disintegration would speed up and there would be the end of it. He wished that he could lose consciousness, that his knees would buckle and he would collapse. He tried with all his might to lose consciousness and collapse. As a child he had been able to do that. He could cry at will; he had been able to hold his breath until he fainted, or hold back his heart for one whole beat. Now he could no longer manage any of it. He simply no longer had himself under control. He could literally no longer bend his knees and crumple. All he could do was just go on standing there, enduring whatever befell him.

Then he heard the soft hum of Monsieur Roedel's limousine. No honking, just that soft, twittery hum that arose when the car's motor had just been started and it was moving out of the back courtyard and toward the entrance. And as this lesser noise broke through to his ear, penetrated his ear and hummed like a jolt of current through every nerve of his body, Jonathan could feel the cracking in his joints and his spine stretching. And he could feel how without any action on his part his extended right leg drew itself toward his left leg, how the left foot pivoted on its heel, how the right knee crooked itself for a step, and then the left, and again the right . . . and how he was placing one foot in front of the other, how, in truth, he was walking, indeed running, how he leaped down the three steps, sped easily to the entrance, opened the grille, stood at attention, smartly put his right hand to the brim of his cap, and let the limousine pass. He did it all completely automatically, without any will of his own, and his conscious mind was a participant only in that it made a thorough inventory of the movements and bustlings. The single original contribution that Jonathan personally made to the event consisted of a wrathful glance and a hail of mute curses with which he pursued Monsieur Roedel's limousine as it glided off.

But then, as he returned to his fixed position, the flames of anger, this last flash of individuality, died within him. And while he mechanically scaled the three steps, the last remnant of his hate ebbed away, and once on top, with eyes no longer spewing venom and rage, he looked down into the street with a kind of broken glance. It seemed to him that these eyes were no longer his own at all, but rather that he was sitting behind his eyes and peering through them as if through dead, round windows; yes, it seemed to him that this whole body enveloping him was no longer his, but that he, Jonathan—or what was left of him—was nothing but a tiny, shrunken gnome inside the gigantic structure of a strange body, a helpless dwarf imprisoned in a human machine grown much too large, much too complicated, one he could no longer control and bend to his own will, but which instead was controlled, if at all, by itself or by some other powers. At the moment it was standing quietly in front of the column—no longer resting within its sphinxlike self, but laid aside or hung up and out of the way like a marionette—and stood there for the last ten minutes of duty still remaining, until at five thirty on the dot Monsieur Vilman appeared at the outer bulletproof glass door for a moment and called "We're closing!" At which, the marionette machine Jonathan Noel set itself in proper motion and went into the bank, placed itself at the control board of the electrical system for locking the doors, switched it on and alternately pressed the two buttons for the inner and outer bulletproof glass doors to let the employees pass through the flood-gates; then, together with Madame Roques, barred the fire doors to the strong room, which had been previously locked by Madame Roques, together with Monsieur Vilman; switched off the electrical system for locking the doors, left the bank together with Madame Roques and Monsieur Vilman and, once Monsieur Vilman had locked the inner and Madame Roques the outer bulletproof glass doors, closed the folding steel gate as per regulation. This done, it made a slight, wooden bow toward Madame Roques and Monsieur Vilman, opened its mouth and bade them a good evening and a fine weekend, received, with expressions of thanks on its part, Monsieur Vilman's best wishes for the weekend and a "Till Monday!" from Madame Roques, waited suitably until the two had moved off several paces, and then filed in with the flow of pedestrians to let them carry it along in the opposite direction.

Walking soothes. There is a healing power in walking. The regular placement of one foot in

front of the other while at the same time row-
ing rhythmically with the arms, the rising rate
of respiration, the slight stimulation of the
pulse, the actions required of eye and ear for
determining direction and maintaining balance, the feeling of the passing air brushing
against the skin—all these are events that
mass about the body and mind in a quite ir-
resistible fashion and allow the soul, be it
ever so atrophied and bruised, to grow and
expand.

Which is what happened to the twofold
Jonathan, to the gnome stuck in the puppet
body much too large for him. Little by little,
step by step, he grew back into his body,
filled it out from the inside, visibly gained
control over it, and finally became one with
it. That was near the corner of the rue du Bac.
And he crossed the rue du Bac (Jonathan the
marionette would surely have turned to the
right, automatically, following his accustomed
path to reach the rue de la Planche) and
ignored the rue Saint-Placide on his left where
his hotel was located and walked straight ahead
as far as the rue de l'Abbé Grégoire, taking

it to the rue de Vaugirard and from there to
the Jardin du Luxembourg. He entered the
park and walked three laps on the outermost,
broadest path, the one joggers used, under the
trees that bordered the railing; then turned to
the south and walked up the boulevard Mont-
parnasse and around the cemetery, once, twice,
and traveling farther west into the Thirteenth
Arrondissement, walked on through the entire
Fifteenth to the Seine, and along the river to
the northeast into the Seventh and then on
into the Sixth, farther and farther—a summer
evening like this knows no end really—and
back to the Luxembourg, where the park was
just being closed as he arrived. At the great
wrought-iron gate to the left of the Senate
building, he halted. It was almost nine o'clock
now, but it was still bright as day all around.
One could deduce the oncoming night only
by a gentle, golden tinge to the light and by
the violet rims of the shadows. The traffic
on the rue de Vaugirard had become thinner,
almost sporadic. The crowds of people had
dispersed. The few small groups of them at

the exits from the parks and at the street corners quickly melted away and vanished one by one into the many narrow streets around Odéon and the church of Saint-Sulpice. People went off to drink an aperitif, to go to a restaurant, to go home. The air was soft with a slight fragrance of flowers. It had grown quiet. Paris was eating.

All at once he noticed how tired he was. His legs, his back, his shoulders hurt from the hours of walking, his feet burned in his shoes. And he was suddenly hungry, so very hungry that his stomach was cramping. He was hungry for soup, for salad and fresh white bread and for a piece of meat. He knew a restaurant, quite close by, on the rue de Canettes, where all of this was to be had as a table d'hôte for forty-seven francs fifty, including service. But he could not go there in this state, sweaty and stinking like this, and with torn trousers.

He set out to walk to his hotel. On the way, in the rue d'Assas, there was a Tunisian grocery. It was still open. He bought a can of sardines, a small piece of goat cheese, a pear, a bottle of red wine, and an Arabian bread.

The hotel room was even smaller than his room on the rue de la Planche, hardly wider at one end than the door you entered by, and at most ten feet long. The walls, to be sure, did not form right angles but—when viewed from the door—veered off from one another until the room had widened to about seven feet, only suddenly to gravitate toward one another and merge in the form of a three-sided apse at the bow. The room had, that is, the outline of a coffin, nor was it much roomier than a coffin. Along one side stood the bed; the washbasin was installed on the other side and beneath it, a bidet that could be swung out. In the apse stood a chair. Above the washbasin on the right, just below the ceiling, a window had been cut out, no more than a little glassed-over vent that gave on an air shaft and could be opened and closed with two cords. A weak, sultry draft entered the coffin through this vent, bearing with it a few very muted sounds from the outside world: the rattle of plates, the whoosh of toilets, shreds of Spanish and Portuguese words, a little laughter, the wailing of a child and sometimes, from very far off, the sound of a car horn.

Perched on the edge of the bed, in his undershirt and underpants, Jonathan ate. He had pulled the chair over to use as a table, placed his cardboard suitcase atop it, and spread the shopping bag over that. He sliced the little sardine bodies lengthwise with his pocketknife, speared a half, spread it over a scrap of bread, and shoved the bite into his mouth. As he chewed, the tender, oil-drenched fish flesh blended with the insipid pita bread into a delicious lump. It lacked perhaps a few drops of lemon, he thought—but this came very close to frivolous gourmandizing, for after each bite, as he took a small swallow of red wine from the bottle, let it run across his tongue and shifted it between his teeth, the steely aftertaste of the fish blended with the lively, acidic bouquet of the wine in such a convincing fashion that Jonathan was certain he had never dined better in all his life than at this very moment. The can held four sardines—that made eight bites, chewed deliberately with the bread, and eight swallows of wine to go with them. He ate very slowly. He had once read in a magazine that eating hurriedly, especially when you were very hungry, was not healthy and could lead to digestive problems, even to nausea and vomiting. He also ate slowly because he believed this meal to be his last.

After he had eaten all the sardines and soaked up the remaining oil from the can with bread, he ate the goat cheese and the pear. The pear was so juicy that it almost slipped from his hands as he peeled it, and the goat cheese was so dense and gummy that it stuck to his knife blade, and it suddenly tasted so acidic-bitter in his mouth that his gums puckered as if in fright and for a moment his saliva dried up. But then the pear, a piece of sweet, dripping pear, and it all started functioning again and blended and came unstuck from his palate and teeth and slid over his tongue and down . . . and another piece of cheese, a mild shock, and again the conciliating pear, and cheese and pear—it tasted so good that he scraped the last remnants of cheese from the paper and ate the wedges of core that he had at first cut away from the fruit.

He sat there for a long while lost in thought, licking his teeth with his tongue, before eating the rest of the bread and drinking the rest of the wine. Then he gathered up the empty can, the peel, the paper from the cheese, wrapped them all up in the shopping bag along with the bread crumbs, deposited the trash and the empty bottle in the corner behind the door, took his suitcase from the chair, put the chair back in its place in the apse, washed his hands and went to bed. He rolled the wool blanket down to the foot of the bed and covered himself with just the sheet. Then he put out the light. It was pitch-dark. Not the least ray of light came into the room, not even from up there where the hatch was; only the weak, sultry draft and the sounds, from far, far off.

It was very humid. "I'll kill myself tomorrow," he said. Then he fell asleep.

That night there was a thunderstorm. It was one of those thunderstorms that do not burst suddenly with a volley of lightning bolts and thunder, but that take a great deal of time and hold back their energies for a long while. For two hours it skulked about indecisively in the sky, with delicate sheet lightning, soft murmurs, shifting from neighborhood to neighborhood as if it didn't know where it should gather its forces, and expanding all the while, it grew and grew, finally covering the entire city like a thin, leaden blanket, waited again, using its irresolution to load itself with even more potent tension, and still it did not break. . . . Nothing moved beneath the blanket. Not the slightest breeze stirred in the sultry air, not a leaf, not a particle of dust, the city lay there as if numbed, it trembled under the crippling tension, as if the city itself were the thunderstorm waiting to erupt into the sky.

And then, finally, as morning was already

approaching and with it a hint of dawn, there was a bang, a single one, as violent as if the whole city were exploding. Jonathan reared up in bed. His conscious mind had not heard the bang, let alone recognized it as a clap of thunder; this was worse: in that second of awakening, it was as if the explosion had coursed like sheer terror through his body, like a terror whose source he did not know, like the fear of death. The only thing that he perceived was the reverberation of the bang, a multiple rumbling, roaring echo of thunder. It sounded as if the houses outside were collapsing like bookcases, and his first thought was: Here we go, this is it, the end. And he did not mean by that simply his own end, but the end of the world, doomsday—an earthquake, the atom bomb, or both—at any rate the absolute end.

But then it was suddenly still as death. No rumbling was to be heard, no toppling, no cracking, no nothing, and no echo of nothing. And this sudden and lasting stillness was more utterly dreadful than the uproar of a doomed world. For now it seemed to Jonathan that, although he himself indeed was still there, except for him nothing else existed, no juxtaposition, no up and down, no outside, no other on which he could have oriented himself. All perception, sight, hearing, sense of balance—everything that could have told him who and where he was—fell away in the perfect vacuum of darkness and stillness. All he could still feel was his own racing heart and the trembling of his body. He knew only that he was in a bed, but not in whose bed, and not where this bed stood—if indeed it stood at all, if it was not falling, toward some unfathomed somewhere, for it seemed to be swaying, and he clutched the mattress with both hands to keep from capsizing, to keep from losing the one something that he held in his hands. He tried to find his footing in the darkness with his eyes, footing in the stillness with his ears, he heard nothing, he saw nothing, absolutely nothing, his stomach rocked, a ghastly taste of sardines rose up in him. Just don't vomit, he thought, just don't throw up, just don't turn yourself inside out now too! . . . and then, after a horrible eternity, he did see something, the tiniest pale shimmer up and to his right, the veriest hint of light. And he stared up at it and held fast to it with his eyes, to a small, square fleck of light, an opening, a border between inside and out, a kind of window in a room . . . but what room? This was certainly not *his* room! "This isn't your room, not on your life! In your room, the window is at the foot of the bed and not so high up toward the ceiling. It isn't . . . it isn't your room in your uncle's house, it's the room you had as a child in your parents' house in Charenton—no, not your room, it's the cellar, yes, you're in the cellar of your parents' house, you're a child, you only dreamed that you had grown up to be a disgusting old guard in Paris, but you're a child and you're sitting in the cellar of your parents' house, and outside is war, and you're trapped, buried, forgotten. Why don't they come? Why don't they rescue me? Why is it so deathly still? Where are the other people? My God, where are the other people? I simply cannot live without other people!"

He was just about to scream. He wanted to

scream this one sentence, that he simply could not live without other people, out into the silence, so great was his agony, so desperate was the fear the aged child Jonathan Noel felt at being abandoned. But in that moment of wanting to scream, he received an answer. He heard a noise.

It was a knock. Very soft. And there was another knock. And a third and a fourth, from somewhere above. And then the knocking shifted into a regular, gentle drumming and the rolling of the drum grew more and more violent, and finally it was no longer drumming, but a powerful, glutted rushing sound, and Jonathan recognized it as the rush of rain.

And at that, the room fell back in order, and now Jonathan recognized the bright, rectangular fleck as the vent to the air shaft, and in the dawning light he recognized the outlines of the hotel room, the washbasin, the chair, the suitcase, the walls.

He released his clutching hold on the mattress, pulled his legs to his chest, and crossed his arms over them. He remained sitting in this crouching position for a good half hour, and listened to the rush of the rain.

Then he stood up and dressed. He didn't need to turn on the light, he found his way about in the twilight. Took suitcase, coat, umbrella and left the room. Softly he descended the stairs. Downstairs, the night porter was sleeping at the reception desk. Jonathan walked over to him on tiptoe and, trying not to wake him, pressed ever so briefly on the button for the door release. It gave a soft click, and the door sprang open. He walked out into the open air.

Out on the street the cool, gray-blue light of morning embraced him. It was no longer raining. It was still dripping from the eaves though and trickling from the awnings and there were puddles on the sidewalks. Jonathan walked down to the rue de Sèvres. There was no one to be seen far and wide and no cars either. The buildings stood, silent and modest, with an almost touching innocence. It was as if the rain had washed away their pride and their pompous luster and all of their menace. Across the way, a cat whisked past the display window of the Bon Marché grocery department and disappeared under the vacated vegetable stands. On the right, at the place Boucicaut, the trees were so wet they crackled. A pair of blackbirds began to whistle, the whistling bounced back off the building facades, further enhancing the stillness that lay over the city.

Jonathan crossed the rue de Sèvres and turned down the rue du Bac, heading home. With every step, his wet soles splashed against the wet asphalt. It's like going barefoot, he thought, and by that he meant more the sound than the slippery sensation of damp in his shoes and socks. He had a great urge to take off his shoes and socks and to walk the rest of the way barefoot, and if he didn't do it, it was only out of laziness and not because he would have found it improper. But he splashed diligently through the puddles, he splashed right through the middle of them, walked in a zigzag from puddle to puddle, sometimes even crossed the street because he saw an especially lovely, wide puddle on the far sidewalk, and stomped through it with flat, splashing soles, sending spray up onto display windows on one side and parked cars on the other and his own trouser legs; it was delightful, he loved making this little childish mess, it was like some great freedom that had been restored to him. And he was still very much traveling on the wings of bliss when he reached the rue de la Planche, entered the building, scurried past Madame Rocard's locked lodge, crossed the back courtyard, and climbed the narrow service stairs.

Only when he was at the top, approaching the seventh floor, did he suddenly become frightened by the end of his journey: up there the pigeon was waiting, that ghastly animal. It would be sitting at the end of the corridor with red, taloned feet, surrounded by dung and drifting wisps of down, and it would brush against him with its wings, impossible to evade in the narrowness of the hallway. . . .

He stopped, and he set his suitcase down, though only five steps still lay ahead of him.

He did not want to turn back. He only wanted to pause for one brief minute, to catch his breath, to let his heart calm down again before he walked this last part of the way.

He looked back. His gaze followed the spiraling oval twists of the railing into the depths of the stairwell, and at every floor he saw the rays of light falling in from the sides. The morning light had lost its blue and grown yellower and warmer, he thought. From the elegant apartments he could hear the first sounds of the awakening house: the tinkle of cups, the muted slam of a refrigerator door, soft radio music. And then suddenly a familiar aroma rushed into his nose, the aroma of Madame Lassalle's coffee, and he sucked in several breathfuls of it, he felt as if he were drinking that coffee. He picked up his suitcase and went on. All at once he was no longer afraid.

As he stepped out into the hall, with a single glance he saw two things right off: the closed window and a cleaning rag that had been laid out to dry over the sink next to the shared toilet. He could not see all the way to the end of the hall; the blinding bright square of light at the window cut off his line of sight. He walked ahead, more or less fearlessly, stepped through the light, entered the shadows behind it. The hall was completely empty. The pigeon had vanished. The splotches on the floor had been wiped away. Not a feather, not a wisp of down left trembling on the red tiles.

A NOTE ON THE TYPE

This book was set on the Linotype in Bodoni Book, named after Giambattista Bodoni (1740–1813), son of a printer of Piedmont. After gaining experience and fame as superintendent of the Press of the Propaganda in Rome, in 1768 Bodoni became the head of the ducal printing house at Parma, which he soon made the foremost of its kind in Europe. His *Manuale Tipografico*, completed by his widow in 1818, contains 279 pages of type specimens, including alphabets of about thirty languages. His editions of Greek, Latin, Italian, and French classics are celebrated for their typography. In type designing he was an innovator, making his new faces rounder, wider, and lighter, with greater openness and delicacy, and with sharper contrast between the thick and thin lines.

Text composition by
Maryland Linotype Composition Company,
Baltimore, Maryland. Display composition
by Heritage Printers, Inc., Charlotte,
North Carolina.

Printed and bound by
The Haddon Craftsmen, Inc.,
Scranton, Pennsylvania

Typography and binding design by
Marysarah Quinn